This book belongs to:

. . . . . . . . . . . . . . . . . . . .

. . . . . . . . . . . . . . . . . . .

For Alexander Deane Cameron, with love.  MM

This paperback edition first published in 2009
by Andersen Press Ltd.
First published in Great Britain in 2008
by Andersen Press Ltd.,
20 Vauxhall Bridge Road, London SW1V 2SA.
Published in Australia
by Random House Australia Pty.,
Level 3, 100 Pacific Highway, North Sydney, NSW 2060.
Text copyright © Miriam Moss, 2008.
Illustration copyright © Jane Simmons, 2008.
The rights of Miriam Moss and Jane Simmons
to be identified as the author and illustrator
of this work have been asserted by them in accordance with
the Copyright, Designs and Patents Act, 1988.
Colour separated in Switzerland by Photolitho AG, Zürich.
Printed and bound in Singapore.

10   9   8   7   6   5   4   3   2   1

British Library Cataloguing in Publication Data available.

ISBN  978 1 84270 758 6

# Matty Takes Off!

Miriam Moss · Jane Simmons

Andersen Press

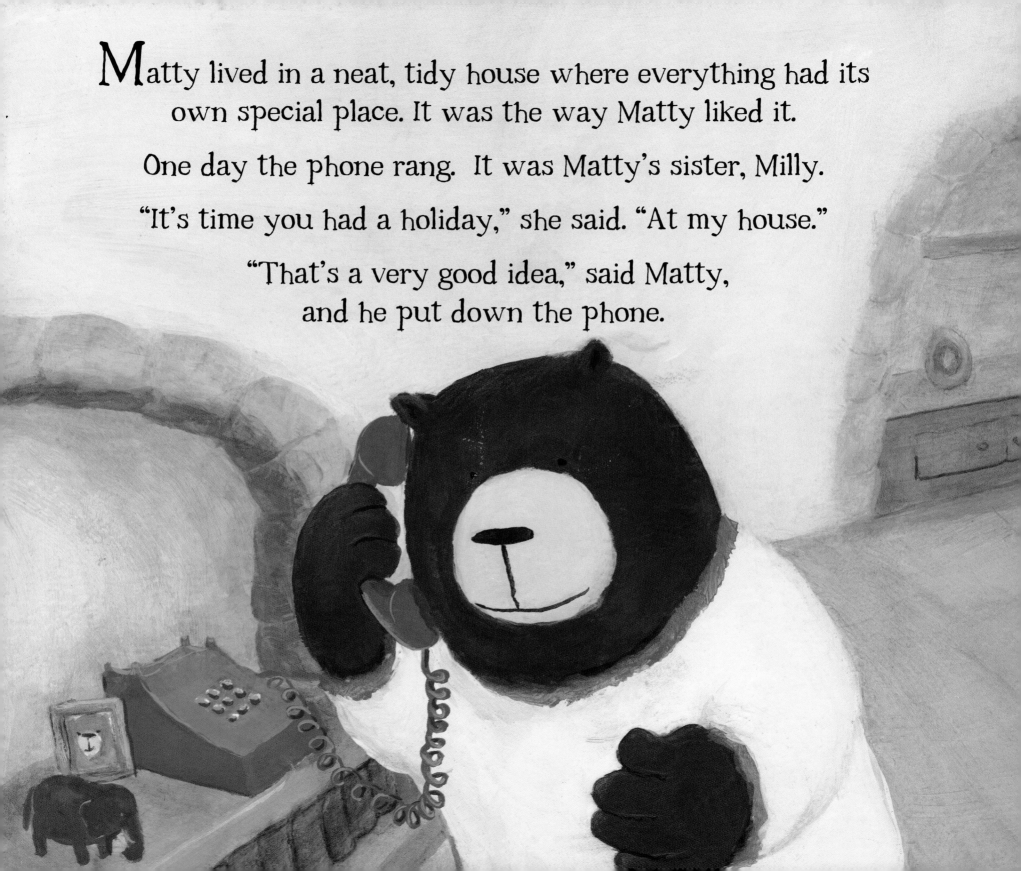

Matty lived in a neat, tidy house where everything had its own special place. It was the way Matty liked it.

One day the phone rang. It was Matty's sister, Milly.

"It's time you had a holiday," she said. "At my house."

"That's a very good idea," said Matty, and he put down the phone.

Matty made a list.

"I'll take a suitcase
of spare clothes,
my tartan coat,
my green leather walking boots,
a packet of my favourite crunchy brunch flakes,
my rainbow mug
and, of course,
Frampton the cat,"
he decided.

Then he gathered everything together and put them neatly on the kitchen table.

Matty went outside and looked lovingly at his old red truck. It was very smart and shiny because he hardly ever used it.

Then he carefully packed all his things into the back of the truck, while Frampton sat waiting on the passenger seat.

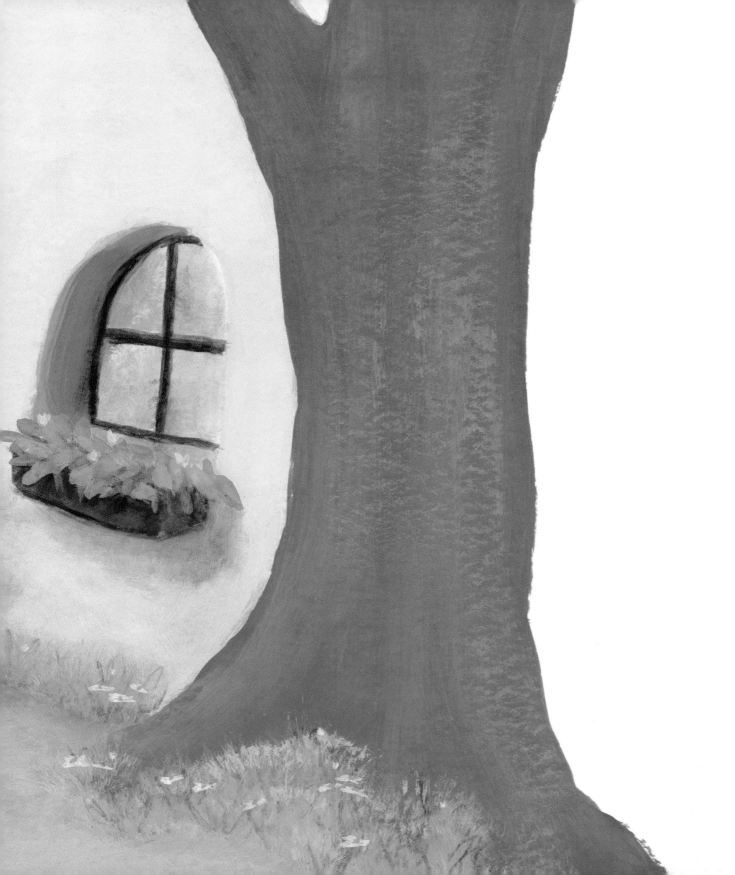

"There,"
said Matty,
climbing in.
"All set and
ready to go."

They set off.

But at the end of the lane
Matty stopped.

He looked worried. Something was missing.

So he reversed the truck, went back into the house and a few minutes later came out, carrying his pillow, duvet and Frampton's woolly rug. He packed them into the back of the truck.

"There," he said, climbing in.
"All set and ready to go."
They set off.

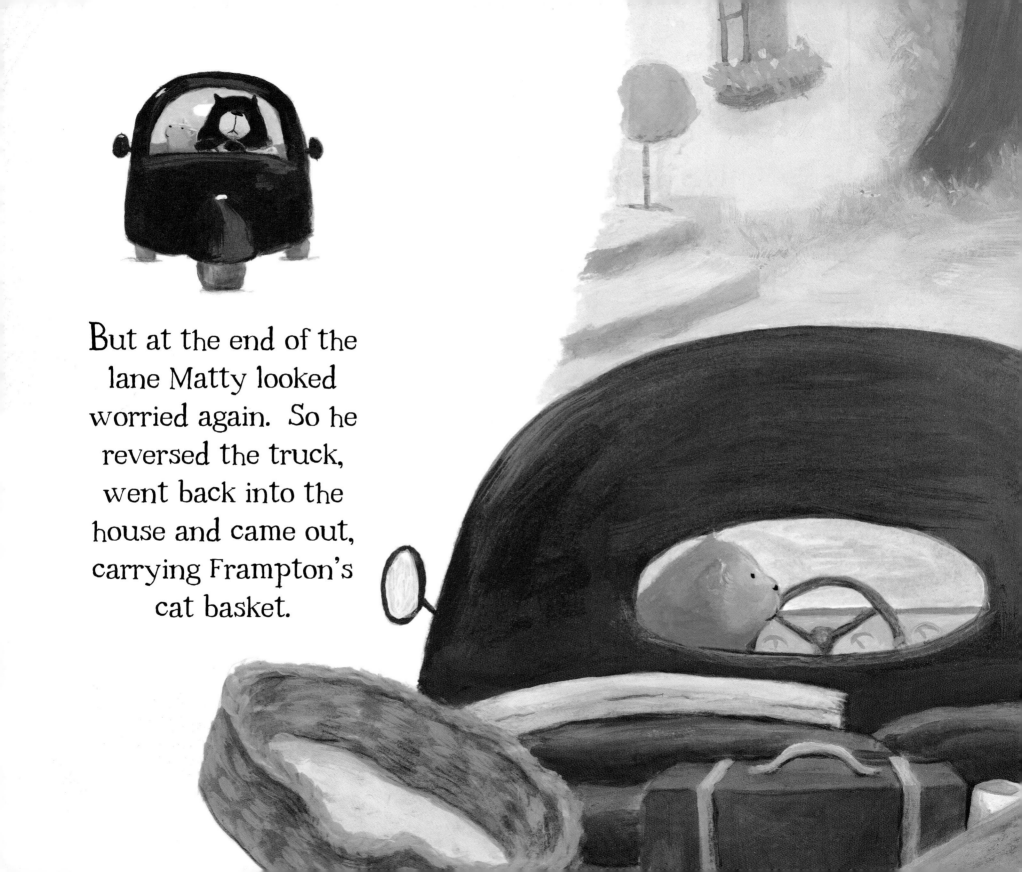

But at the end of the
lane Matty looked
worried again. So he
reversed the truck,
went back into the
house and came out,
carrying Frampton's
cat basket.

Then he went back into the house again.
Frampton sat patiently listening to the hammering
coming from the house. Soon Matty came out, carrying
his bed-in-bits and a floppy mattress and added
them to the things in the truck. By now,
the truck was quite full.

"There," said Matty. "Now we
really *are* all set and ready to go."

"But what if it rains?" said Matty.
He got out again.

Matty came out of the house,
carrying a big tarpaulin.

He fought with it,
until it was firmly tied down
over the back of the truck.

"All set and ready to go?" Matty asked Frampton.

Frampton looked sideways at him and said nothing.

They bumped and bounced down to the end of the lane.

This time Matty looked DETERMINED. He swung left and out on the open road! Matty began to feel so pleased with himself that he started to sing:

"We're out on the open road,
With a great big wobbling load.
A bed and some boots,
Oh, who gives two hoots,
We're out on the open road."

Frampton joined in.

Matty and Frampton were enjoying the song so much that they didn't notice the tarpaulin flapping.

The flaps got bigger

and bigger

and bigger.

With nothing holding it down, the floppy mattress somersaulted off the back of the truck and hit the ground.

FLUMP!

"Oh, who gives two hoots! We're out on the open road."

Then the wind sucked the bits-of-bed out of the truck.
Schlooooop!

Whoosh!
went Frampton's woolly rug.

Flip!
went Matty's coat.

Fwish!
went his cereal.

Zip!
went Frampton's basket.

Crash!
went his painted mug.

A stream of clothes shot into the air and an
empty suitcase bounced away down the hill.

Poom!
went his pillow.

Whizz!
went his walking boots.

Fllooosh!
went his duvet.

Faster and faster went the
truck. Louder and louder
sang Matty and Frampton,

until they stopped outside a tall, pink house.

Matty's sister trotted down the steps to greet them.
"No luggage?" she said, looking into the truck.
Matty and Frampton turned round.
The back of the truck yawned emptily at them.

That night, Matty
(wearing a pair of his
sister's pink pyjamas)
snuggled down in bed.
The bed was soft,
the duvet sweet and
Frampton purred
on his feet.

Matty's sister was busy cleaning her teeth,
when she heard something . . .

What she heard was a carefree bear singing:

purrrrrr

# Also available:

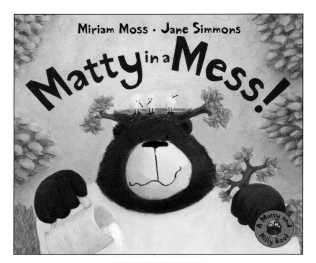

Miriam Moss · Jane Simmons

Matty in a Mess!

A Matty and Milly Book

ISBN 9781842708125